Marion Public Library
1095 6th Avenue
Marion, IA 52302-3428
(319) 377-3412

Itchy Pig

Written by Nicole Bruno Cox
Illustrations by Jessie Judge

INKSHARES

Itchy Pig author Nicole Cox's life changed when she and her husband adopted Gunner, a rescued pit bull puppy who had suffered abuse and neglect at the hands of his former owners. With his short, tattered ears and large snout, he resembled a cute little pig, and because Gunner suffers from food and outdoor seasonal allergies, he was always itchy! So they started calling him "Itchy Pig," and the nickname stuck. After experimenting with different foods, Nicole found some that Gunner wasn't allergic to—fruits and veggies are his favorite treats—and the sick puppy has now grown into a healthy and happy dog. Gunner's story inspired Nicole to write a children's book to help kids learn about allergies and how to live with them.

For my husband, Ronald "Aldo" Cox. You are my rock, utmost fan, and best friend; because of you anything is possible.

–Nicole

To my husband for your endless encouragement and for gladly stepping in to play the role of "momma"; and to my daughter, who has given me a deeper desire to do and be more.

–Jessie

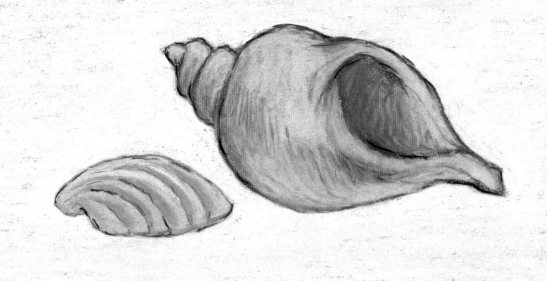

Itchy Pig loves his playtime outdoors.

He likes mountains and parks and bright beachy shores.

"Oh, Itchy Pig, dear!" his mom likes to say.

"Remember that allergies might cause you dismay."

But Itchy Pig turns
and decides to ignore,

while leaving the barn to
go out and explore.

"This sure is fun!" he shouts as he runs,

while flowers and butterflies dance in the sun.

Itchy Pig's happy—so full of glee.

He's oblivious to hazards
he just cannot see.

Now sniffling and scratching
with all of his might,

Itchy Pig thinks: Mom just may be right!

With watery eyes and a throat-catching wheeze,
Itchy Pig sneezes a very big sneeze.

"Mom!" he squeals,
seeking hugs in alarm.

"Oh, Itchy Pig, dear, the
plants mean no harm."

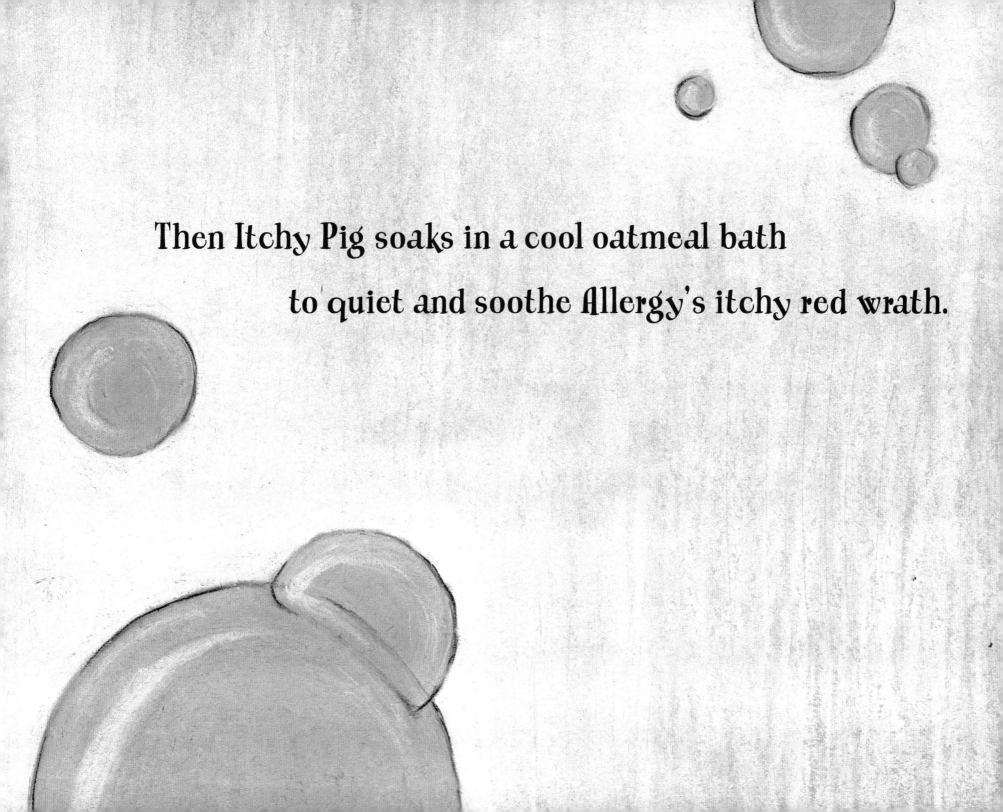

Then Itchy Pig soaks in a cool oatmeal bath

to quiet and soothe Allergy's itchy red wrath.

"Don't worry, my boy, you surely will heal.
And with all of our love, the better you'll feel."

Itchy Pig sighs and soon becomes calm.

He does know it's best to listen to Mom.

So Itchy Pig strives to become more aware.

Before playing outside, he always prepares.

He now understands his outdoor surroundings.

Nature's not scary—it's rather astounding.

Of course Itchy Pig still can be rather headstrong
as his mom helps point out all his rights and his wrongs.

"Oh, Itchy Pig, dear–it's raining and pouring!
It's not the best time for your outdoor exploring!"

Published by Inkshares, Inc., San Francisco, California

www.inkshares.com

Edited and designed by Girl Friday Productions
www.girlfridayproductions.com
Cover design by Paul Barrett
Illustrations by Jessie Judge

ISBN: 9781941758571
e-ISBN: 9781941758588
Library of Congress Control Number: 2015942972

10 9 8 7 6 5 4 3 2 1

First edition 2016. Printed by RR Donnelley.

Printed in China

List of Patrons

This book was made possible in part by the following grand patrons who preordered the book on Inkshares.com. Thank you.

Adair Andreasson
Allison G. Anderson
Anne Edgerton Pajel
Ann Marie Hosek
Ashley L. Sewell
Azure and Ben
Bonnie Lawton
Bryan Judge
Carol J. Cox
Charlotte Page Rorech
Crystal G. Frye
Dan and Kristi Holman
Deborah Stallings
Dianna M. Bruno
Dustin R. Vail
Eddie Riddell
Elaina B. Farmer

Emma B. Turner
Erica L. Pigage
Faith and Phil Leverett
Frank B. Bruno
George T. Fore
Harrison Burch
Heather Greene
Janice Holbrook
Jennifer M. Johnson
Jessica J. Judge
Joseph Judge
J. F. Cicci
Karla Steele
Katelynn Ruth Dortch
Katherine Minguez
Kathie Laulette
Keaton B. Hanselman

Kristen Saidla
Lindsey Harris
Lisa Campbell
Luis and Rachel
Marilyn M. Miller
Megan M. Berrio
Michael R. Goede
Mr. Graham Vann
Myra Lee Gerard
Nancy A. Robinson
Natalie A. Cherry
Nicholas Kottlowski
Paul M. Bruno
Phil Kim
Reb
Renee M. DeGeorge
Richard Coull

Ronald Cox
Ron and Lory Bruno
Ron Cox
Sarah K. Oden
Sara Price
Smith Classroom
Sophie Sims
Stephanie Z. Horton
Tara Whalen
Teresa S. Klingenstein
Tyler Johnson

Inkshares

Inkshares is a crowdfunded book publisher. We democratize publishing by having readers select the books we publish—we edit, design, print, distribute, and market any book that meets a pre-order threshold.

Interested in making a book idea come to life? Visit inkshares.com to find new book projects or to start your own.